ISABEL: THE FORGOTTEN DAUGHTER OF LA LLORONA

ALSO BY ARTHUR MILLS

The Empty Lot Next Door

The Crawl Space

Friend or Foe

Co-Author

Candle Face Chronicles: The Lost Souls [Book One]

Candle Face Chronicles: The Lost Souls [Book Two]

The Haunted Handbook: Forms and Strategies for Paranormal Investigations

The Legend of Mara Flores

ISABEL: THE FORGOTTEN DAUGHTER OF LA LLORONA

CANDLE FACE CHRONICLES: BOOK THREE

MR. SMOE

ARTHUR MILLS

BRANCHING PLOT BOOKS

To my readers,

This new account, Isabel, is dedicated to you, the ones who sift through every hidden clue, determined to piece together Candle Face's origins. Just as you brought curiosity to the Lost Souls before, now you must turn your eyes to Isabel's story and search for what connects her to Candle Face.

Every note you examine, every variation you consider, holds a piece of the puzzle. Each hint might bring us closer to stopping Candle Face once and for all. Your attention to overlooked details and willingness to question everything is essential. Without it, we may never find the key to her downfall.

I ask you to bring the same courage you showed in The Lost Souls. Keep your mind open, and let empathy guide you as you work through Isabel's fate.

Thank you for standing with me in this investigation. Together, we can connect the pieces of Candle Face's past and take another step toward her defeat. Your commitment to this book's interactive nature gives us all a fighting chance to stop her.

ISABEL

Beneath a moon's grieving glow, an infant gasped for breath,
Her father's hands once held her close, then fate conspired with death.
Laughter danced through fleeting days, then silence came too soon,
A mother's wail split through the dark and drowned beneath the moon.

The river's pace was swift and cold, three souls pulled far below,
But history lost a daughter's name: erased, unloved, unknown.
Her brothers rose to godhood's heights, their voices scorched the sky,
Yet when she called, their voices mocked and left her soul to die.

A trickster's hand reached through the dark, his voice carved out her fate,
With fire's kiss, he burned her name and left her bound in hate.
She rose from ash with hollow eyes, her touch a brand of pain,
No mercy left, no past to claim, just suffering engraved in flame.

She called her name in tongues long lost, the wind refused to speak,
Her hands, once small, now shaped the void where vengeance makes its keep.
She built her legions, watched them burn, the faithful turned to dust,
Their voices sang, their bodies fell, devotion bred in rust.

Now through the night, she walks unseen, lost souls bend to her will,
In every telling, her fate remains — her name, Candle Face, haunts us still.

KEY TO UNDERSTANDING

If you're new to the *Candle Face Chronicles*, or if you haven't explored the earlier books, I encourage you to start with *The Empty Lot Next Door*. Inspired by real ghostly events in Austin, Texas, my award-winning memoir offers the first glimpses of Candle Face's presence and the trauma that followed.

From there, the *Candle Face Chronicles* expand the investigation. In *The Lost Souls [Book One]* and *[Book Two]*, you'll help locate the remains of Candle Face's victims and track those who kill for her.

Reading these books before *Isabel* will give you a stronger sense of Candle Face's power and the story that now centers on Isabel's long-buried past. Each book stands on its own, but together they tell a larger story of betrayal and secrets.

With *Isabel*, the investigation continues. Every note, every variant, every buried clue brings us closer to understanding Candle Face's past and stopping what she has planned. The puzzle is vast, but what we've already discovered will make your time in Isabel's world that much more complete.

The Empty Lot Next Door
- Paperback: https://amzn.to/46lCovb
- eBook for Kindle: https://amzn.to/44YFww4
- Audiobook: https://amzn.to/40RIHH1

Candle Face Chronicles: The Lost Souls [Book One]
- Paperback: https://amzn.to/4dz3m7d
- eBook for Kindle: https://amzn.to/4bsM6ib

Candle Face Chronicles: The Lost Souls [Book Two]
- Paperback: https://amzn.to/4jAhbVS
- eBook for Kindle: https://amzn.to/40Avzoh

READING INSTRUCTIONS

Welcome to *Isabel*, an interactive reading experience built from the cryptic notes of Mr. Smoe, a devout Candle Face Disciple. In most interactive stories, you jump between numbered pages. Here, you pick different versions of individual notes, shaping Isabel's story note by note. By flipping each note, you uncover new variants of the same moment, shifting relationships, altering motives, and changing events in small but dramatic ways.

How to Flip Each Note

1. **Find the Right Book** – Isabel is divided into eleven volumes: Book One, Book Two, and so on, up to Book Eleven.

2. **Identify the Note** – In each Book, there's essentially one "page" containing eight notes, arranged in horizontal rows. Each note can appear in eight possible variants, labeled A through H.

3. **Pick a Variant** – For Note 1, choose one letter (A–H). For Note 2, pick another, and so forth until you reach Note 8. These eight choices form your unique reading of that Book.

Understanding the Numbering System

Mr. Smoe's original filing system was chaotic, so I developed a simple system to track each variant:

[Book Number] – [Note Number] – [Variant Letter]

For example, "6-3-H" means:

- **6** → Book Six

- **3** → Note 3

- **H** → The H variant of that Note

This system helps you keep track of different readings and compare variations.

Exploring the Possibilities

With just eight notes per book and each note offering eight variants, that's 16,777,216 possible ways to read just one Book. At three minutes per combination, it could take around 95 years of constant reading to exhaust all variants of one Book. Across all eleven Books, the total climbs to approximately 2.96×10^{79} readings, a number so large that reading them all would take far longer than the age of our universe.

Good Luck

Thank you for joining this mission to investigate Isabel's past and her transformation into Candle Face. What we learn improves our chances of stopping Candle Face's plans. Keep flipping, keep reading, and let every variant bring you closer to the answers we need.

CUTTING INSTRUCTIONS

This paperback version of *Isabel* is different from the original spiral-bound edition. In the spiral version, each note was precut, allowing readers to flip between variants easily. Unfortunately, Amazon doesn't offer spiral-bound printing with precut pages, so in this edition, you'll need to prepare the pages yourself.

To fully engage with *Isabel's* interactive structure, you must cut between each note before reading. This allows you to lift and flip individual notes as intended. Please follow the instructions below carefully.

How to Cut Each Page

1. Locate the Dotted Lines
   Each "book" contains eight pages. Each page has eight horizontal notes, separated by dotted lines. Between these notes, you'll see dotted cut lines running from the **far-right margin** toward the inner part of the page.

2. Use Scissors Only
   Carefully cut along each dotted line, starting at the far-right edge of the paper. Continue just slightly past the end of the dotted line, stopping just before the inner gutter. If the cut doesn't reach the edge or strays off line, the strips on the next page may catch or misalign. Precision matters. The better the cut, the better the understanding.

   Important: The dotted lines stop short of the page edges due to printing limitations, but your cuts should not. Begin at the far-right edge of the paper and continue just slightly past the end of the dotted line – stopping just before the inner gutter. Do not cut all the way through. You're creating slits, not removing sections. The left margin holds each note in place for flipping. Clean, even cuts are essential. The better the cut, the better the understanding, and the closer you may get to the secrets the Aztec gods never meant to be found.

3. **Cut One Page at a Time** *(Highly Recommended)*
   Don't cut multiple pages at once. Some pages, like the title page at the beginning of each new book, aren't meant to be cut and contain no dotted lines. Stacking pages while cutting increases the risk of damaging these sections.

4. **Make Seven Cuts Per Note Page**

   Each page contains eight stacked notes. That means you'll make **seven horizontal cuts** between them.

5. **Test the Flip, Then Tuck if Needed**

   After cutting, gently flip a single note upward. If it springs back down, you can fold the flap down softly at the base to help it stay lifted while you read. A slight crease is enough to improve movement without weakening the paper. Remember, this is an active investigation. You're not just flipping paper, you're searching for clues about Isabel's life. It's not supposed to be easy. But nothing worth uncovering ever is.

Paperback vs. Premium Spiral Edition

If you'd prefer a version that arrives fully prepared, a **precut premium spiral edition** is available at: **https://candleface.com/pages/isabel-the-forgotten-daughter-of-la-llorona**

This premium version:

- Lays completely flat for easy flipping

- Is precut and ready to explore

- Includes an authentication sticker to confirm it's an official copy

- Is hand-numbered in the order it was created

- Takes over three hours to assemble by hand

It's the most seamless and interactive way to experience *Isabel: The Forgotten Daughter of La Llorona.*

But don't discount the paperback. This version:

- Is more affordable and widely available

- Appeals to readers who enjoy a hands-on role in the investigation

- Is easy to travel with or annotate

- Serves as a great secondary copy for testing variant paths

- And let's face it, cutting it yourself feels just a little forbidden

A Final Note

These instructions might sound like a lot of trouble. Maybe they are.
But what you're holding was never meant to be easy.

Isabel's story was scattered, torn apart, nearly erased. To hear it properly, you'll need to cut through the silence yourself.

These are pieces of a past the Aztec gods wanted forgotten.
Every cut opens a moment Isabel once lived. Every lifted note brings you closer to the pieces she left behind.

Some say the story changes depending on who holds the book.
But maybe it doesn't change at all.
Maybe you'll be the one to find the secrets – and finally solve one of the oldest mysteries the world tried to forget.

Whatever you believe, cut with care.
She's waited a long time to be read.

INTRODUCTION

Some readers may be familiar with "Mr. Smoe" from my earlier writings, but here's a brief note for those who aren't. Mr. Smoe was a devoted Candle Face Disciple who passed away, leaving me three boxes filled with peculiar scraps: napkins, gum wrappers, and bits of paper scrawled with cryptic notes. At first, I dismissed them as scattered thoughts. Then I realized they formed a massive puzzle tied to Candle Face and to a figure named Isabel.

As I pieced together these notes, a story began to emerge. It traces Isabel's life from her origins to her transformation into Candle Face. What you're about to read is the version I reconstructed.

Isabel is divided into eleven "books," or chapters, each containing eight pages with eight notes. Each note has eight variations, creating 16,777,216 possible versions of a single book. At three minutes per reading, it would take about 95 years, reading day and night, to experience every combination of just that one book.

But there's more. Combining all eleven books yields approximately 2.96×10^{79} total readings, an 80-digit number so large it has no common name. At three minutes per variant, you would need approximately 1.69×10^{74} years to attempt them all, far exceeding the universe's lifespan.

So why attempt this at all? Because these notes may hold the key to defeating Candle Face. Each variant uncovers a new thread in the betrayals that shaped Isabel's life and afterlife. What we learn improves our chances of stopping Candle Face for good. Mr. Smoe's records aren't perfect, and my assembly and labeling may be flawed, but together we can sift through every note and variation to discover what we need to end Candle Face's power.

Whether you're new to Mr. Smoe's legacy or have followed this investigation from the start, approach *Isabel* with a sharp eye. A single altered note may shift Isabel's motives and expose another side of her family's fate. By sharing what we discover, we might push Candle Face one step closer to losing her power and give Isabel the resolution she was denied.

BOOK ONE

BIRTH BENEATH THE WEEPING MOON

16,777,216 ways to witness a fragile birth

Dawn was hours away, though the moon offered a pale glow near a calm lake.

1-1-A

Inside that abode, a mother fought exhaustion yet found strength for a final push.

1-2-A

Father arrived just in time, carrying a small pouch of maize and a single earthen figurine.

1-3-A

Neighbors gathered at a respectful distance, eager for news yet mindful of the family's space.

1-4-A

Mother cradled the infant, tears in her gaze, yet a spark of calm settled in her chest.

1-5-A

Midwives wiped sweat from mother's brow, reminding her to rest before the next day's tasks.

1-6-A

Few noticed how the moon seemed to shed faint tears across the water's surface.

1-7-A

Finally, mother closed her eyes, drawn into a rare sleep free of looming sorrow.

1-8-A

A slight breeze nudged reed huts along a winding shore, carrying traces of roasted maize.

1-1-B

She clenched a woven blanket, eyes locked on the tiny life waiting to emerge.

1-2-B

He bowed near the mat, relief lighting his features at the sound of new life.

1-3-B

Clay cups of water were offered, a small token of support from watchful relatives.

1-4-B

The child's breathing slowed, as if the gentle torchlight lulled every flicker of worry.

1-5-B

An elder measured the infant's length, muttering an old phrase about strong lineage.

1-6-B

Somewhere far off, an omen could have stirred, but this hut remained a haven for now.

1-7-B

The father lingered a moment longer, quietly thanking the night for this small grace.

1-8-B

Stars flickered overhead, as if pausing to watch an event within those clay walls.

1-1-C

Midwives steadied her arms, each breath carrying her toward relief.

1-2-C

Wrapped in a cotton mantle, he set his spear aside to kneel beside mother and child.

1-3-C

A neighbor hummed a tune, soft enough to calm the newborn's short cries.

1-4-C

Father brushed aside a stray ember from the hearth, focused on the soft coo from his daughter.

1-5-C

A mild aroma of herbs drifted from the corner, meant to ward off foul spirits.

1-6-C

No sign of conflict touched these walls, though hushed voices outside spoke of trouble brewing.

1-7-C

A wave of relief swept over the family, each person clinging to the newborn's first hours.

1-8-C

Lanterns by a beaten path cast shifting patterns on the earthen ground.

1-1-D

A shallow bowl of water stood ready, reflecting her face etched with determination.

1-2-D

Over long journeys he had seen strife, yet this moment outshone every hardship.

1-3-D

Someone brought fresh linens, dyed with simple patterns that brightened the dim hut.

1-4-D

A calm hush replaced earlier tension, letting each family member release a burden.

1-5-D

One relative recounted how the moon foretold fortune for children born under its silver hue.

1-6-D

A stray gust rattled the door, a small reminder that peace can be fragile.

1-7-D

In that shelter, dawn seemed a distant concept, yet hearts felt lighter than before.

1-8-D

Low drumming from a distant camp set a quiet pulse in the cool night air.

1-1-E

Sweat beaded her brow, and gentle chants rose, urging her onward.

1-2-E

Gently, he placed a woven cloth by their side, an emblem of home and unity.

1-3-E

Laughter mixed with hushed relief, forming a gentle lull in the once-tense air.

1-4-E

Linens and lullabies carried them through the first minutes of parenthood.

1-5-E

Ashes in a small bowl hinted at a cleansing rite, though no one hurried to perform it.

1-6-E

Mother breathed deep, choosing to believe only in the child's soft warmth tonight.

1-7-E

Time inched forward, each breath a gentle tie to a fresh start.

1-8-E

Torches flickered across a small clearing, marking the humble home at its center.

1-1-F

She prayed for a child free from strife, even as pain rippled through her frame.

1-2-F

A trembling grin touched his face, for he sensed more than mere chance in this birth.

1-3-F

Midwives shared stories of past births, each a testament to life's unbroken thread.

1-4-F

Though exhaustion weighed on mother's limbs, a gentle pride lit her face.

1-5-F

Light from a single lantern revealed each tired smile, a silent vow of unity.

1-6-F

A cousin glanced at the fading stars, suspecting this calm might not last forever.

1-7-F

Outside, the moon slowly yielded to the night as if granting them room to dream.

1-8-F

The moon hung heavy, reflecting on shallow waters that seemed to hold a secret sorrow.

1-1-G

Tension held the air, but a spark of hope shone in her weary gaze.

1-2-G

He touched the child's forehead with care, hoping the night carried blessing rather than grief.

1-3-G

Small gifts lined the corner: a clay rattle, a handful of herbs, and a scrap of woven cloth.

1-4-G

They took turns holding the newborn, marveling at tiny features that promised a new dawn.

1-5-G

An infant's quiet breath rose above any distant drumbeat, anchoring the family in the present.

1-6-G

In the quiet, father's gaze clouded for a moment, as if recalling some distant regret.

1-7-G

No grand celebration was planned, but love filled the space like a quiet festival.

1-8-G

Soft silhouettes brushed the horizon, hinting that morning might bring both relief and doubt.

1-1-H

At last, a newborn cry rang out, strong enough to stir every corner of that humble room.

1-2-H

Though fear lurked in his heart, he chose to celebrate this fragile joy.

1-3-H

Faces shone with cautious delight, uncertain how long this peace would hold.

1-4-H

With each passing moment, relief grew, as if no calamity could break this circle.

1-5-H

The father stood watch near the door, half-expecting a sudden storm or unsettled dream.

1-6-H

Yet each heartbeat in that room sounded like a promise no storm could shatter.

1-7-H

At least for this night, life tasted sweet, and shadows held no power here.

1-8-H

BOOK TWO

DAYS OF SUNLIT LAUGHTER

16,777,216 glimpses of brief innocence

At dawn, sunlight danced on reed rooftops, hinting at a day brimming with simple delights.

2-1-A

Isabel trotted beside her two younger brothers, each racing through tall grass without a care.

2-2-A

The father paused from patching a broken net, observing his children with quiet pride.

2-3-A

Mother hummed a cheery tune while laying out damp clothes on a sunbaked stone.

2-4-A

Neighbors passed by with kind waves, heading to the main road for the morning bustle.

2-5-A

Midday arrived, and the family gathered under a simple awning for a modest feast.

2-6-A

The children grabbed small fishing rods, dashing to the shore to test their luck.

2-7-A

By sunset, the siblings returned with small fish and even bigger smiles, arms linked in victory.

2-8-A

A mild breeze stirred the lake's surface, creating soft ripples that caught children's eyes.

2-1-B

They giggled over tiny fish darting near the water's edge, untroubled by any distant gloom.

2-2-B

He waved them over to taste fresh grilled maize, a simple treat he'd prepared with care.

2-3-B

She offered slices of ripe fruit to each child, relishing their bright-eyed thanks.

2-4-B

A visiting merchant brought clay trinkets, which made the boys gasp with wide-eyed wonder.

2-5-B

Steaming tortillas passed from hand to hand, each bite tasting of love and easy conversation.

2-6-B

A few friends tagged along, turning the expedition into a lively contest of skill.

2-7-B

Lanterns soon lit the humble paths, revealing a day's worth of footprints etched in dust.

2-8-B

Smoke from cooking fires drifted upward, blending with the glow of early morning rays.

2-1-C

She showed them how to skip stones, delighting when one skimmed the surface three times.

2-2-C

A chuckle rumbled in his chest when the boys boasted about catching the biggest fish someday.

2-3-C

Her soft laugh carried across the yard whenever one of the boys tripped over a playful pup.

2-4-C

Giggling friends nudged Isabel to join them in a quick game of tossing pebbles into a bucket.

2-5-C

The boys bragged of future quests while Isabel teased them, her grin never fading.

2-6-C

Isabel guided her younger brothers across slick stones, mindful that a slip could drench them, or worse.

2-7-C

Night air cooled sweaty brows, though no heart felt weary enough to regret this busy day.

2-8-C

Birds fluttered past clay walls, bringing a gentle chorus that eased every soul awake.

2-1-D

All three dashed around a patch of wildflowers, turning the field into a playful maze.

2-2-D

He called Isabel to help sort a small pile of dried peppers, praising her steady hands.

2-3-D

Isabel lingered at her side, learning how to grind maize kernels for the day's meal.

2-4-D

The air rang with cheerful banter, each greeting a small sign that this community thrived.

2-5-D

Mother smiled softly, refilling cups of water from a clay pitcher to keep everyone refreshed.

2-6-D

Sunlight sparkled off the ripples, each shimmer lifting spirits another notch.

2-7-D

A hush settled across the village, but echoes of fun still hovered near each doorway.

2-8-D

Crisp air carried hints of fresh tortillas, a reminder that daily tasks were underway.

2-1-E

Gentle sunbeams lit their carefree shouts, bonding them in an hour of pure harmony.

2-2-E

Nearby, he sharpened a tool against a smooth stone, glancing up to ensure they stayed safe.

2-3-E

A basket of herbs awaited her sorting, each leaf meant for soothing any future ache.

2-4-E

An elder stopped to admire the siblings, noting that laughter kept spirits strong.

2-5-E

A moment of quiet settled as they savored the meal, connected by warmth instead of words.

2-6-E

Nets cast earlier fluttered in the breeze, waiting for a hopeful catch by dusk.

2-7-E

The father paused at the threshold, a faint concern crossing his features for an instant.

2-8-E

Colorful threads hung outside each hut, set to dry in the first warmth of the day.

2-1-F

A brief tumble brought laughter, proof that minor scrapes could never dim their fun.

2-2-F

Gentle satisfaction glowed on his face; these small tasks felt vital to their family's peace.

2-3-F

She brushed stray hair from Isabel's face, calling that the day felt blessed indeed.

2-4-F

Friendly chatter erupted when a stray dog wove between legs, seeking scraps and pats.

2-5-F

After eating, they dozed in a patch of shade, content to let the sun keep its vigil.

2-6-F

Father stayed behind, mending a broken basket with sure hands but thoughtful eyes.

2-7-F

Mother folded worn cloths, recalling a moment when sorrow once lurked closer than she'd admit.

2-8-F

Sparks of brightness shone off small canals, guiding neighbors to the plaza for trade.

2-1-G

They tested their balance along a narrow log, each step fueling boisterous cheer.

2-2-G

Now and then, he glanced at the horizon, as if measuring how much time they had left together.

2-3-G

Outside tasks could wait, she decided, for her children's glee mattered most this morning.

2-4-G

The father traded a handful of peppers for a sweet cake, delighting the children at once.

2-5-G

Father cleaned up stray crumbs, proud that not a single morsel went to waste.

2-6-G

The mother watched from afar, content that joy filled these hours despite chores undone.

2-7-G

Isabel tucked the younger boys in, her protective nature shining more with each year.

2-8-G

All around, humble smiles greeted the dawn, as though night's worries no longer mattered.

2-1-H

When a small frog hopped by, the siblings paused in awe, a shared grin on each face.

2-2-H

He set aside worries of trade deals and joined their game, clumsy but grinning wide.

2-3-H

In the warmth of the midday sun, she paused to remember a time when sorrow loomed larger.

2-4-H

No harsh tone cut through these lanes; even old grudges lay dormant under such bright skies.

2-5-H

Even the dogs lazed nearby, lulled by full bellies and the midday haze.

2-6-H

In that golden stretch, laughter felt unstoppable, casting aside all hints of future clouds.

2-7-H

Tomorrow might shift fortunes, yet for now, they let these sunlit memories soothe every care.

2-8-H

BOOK THREE

SHADES OF ISOLATION

16,777,216 vantage points on growing loneliness

Morning light crept across the yard, yet Isabel sensed a hush in the air she hadn't felt before.

3-1-A

Mother fussed over the two boys, praising every small feat as though it were heroic.

3-2-A

Father rose early these days, grabbing tools and leaving before dawn fully broke.

3-3-A

The boys boasted about wrestling or fishing, while neighbors admired their energy.

3-4-A

She replayed old memories of fun, hoping to feel the laughter that once came so easily.

3-5-A

The father's late returns sparked quiet talk among neighbors, though nobody addressed Isabel.

3-6-A

Friends who once invited Isabel along now seemed to greet her brothers first.

3-7-A

Day by day, the gap between Isabel and her kin widened, forming cracks none addressed.

3-8-A

The sun rose like always, but her heart noticed a change she could not name.

3-1-B

The boys dashed about, urged on by mother's applause, while Isabel hung back.

3-2-B

He spoke fewer words, a distant look crossing his face whenever Isabel caught his eye.

3-3-B

Each new plan they announced drew father's approval, fueling their confidence.

3-4-B

A knot formed in her stomach whenever mother's proud gaze focused on the boys alone.

3-5-B

Some said a new trading route promised better fortune but also more absence at home.

3-6-B

She strolled alone by the riverside, recalling how group outings once included her laugh.

3-7-B

Father's return on a stormy evening brought stiff silence, mother's eyes flickering with anger.

3-8-B

Neighbors carried on with chores, though Isabel's mood lingered in a dim place.

3-1-C

She laid fresh fruit on the table, ignoring Isabel's small offer to help.

3-2-C

Faint lines on his brow hinted at worries he chose not to share with her.

3-3-C

Isabel watched from a step away, curious yet unable to join their circle.

3-4-C

She tried to stay busy, yet a hollow space in her heart only deepened.

3-5-C

A traveling relative mentioned father's interest in another woman, fueling silent speculation.

3-6-C

The boys joined lively games in the village square, with mother cheering close by.

3-7-C

The boys' jokes fell flat as mother refused to speak, leaving Isabel uncertain where she stood.

3-8-C

A gentle breeze brushed the reed walls, offering little comfort to her restless mind.

3-1-D

Each laugh aimed at the boys stung Isabel more, forming a silent ache.

3-2-D

At meals, he hailed the boys' bold ideas but barely met Isabel's glance.

3-3-D

Mother doted on their stories, paying little attention to Isabel's small comments.

3-4-D

Some nights, she couldn't sleep, mind tangled in questions about her own place.

3-5-D

Rumors swirled of father seeking deals in far villages, leaving mother on edge.

3-6-D

An emptiness followed Isabel as she noted father rarely paused to hear her thoughts.

3-7-D

A fragile hush weighed on the household, as if one spark could destroy their uneasy peace.

3-8-D

Gone were the days of boundless glee, replaced by low spirits she tried to hide.

3-1-E

Though mother still smiled at her, that spark of closeness felt less certain.

3-2-E

Sometimes he stayed away late, returning after the children were half-asleep.

3-3-E

Even passing traders noticed the boys, calling them spirited lads with bright futures.

3-4-E

Her reflection in still water revealed a girl seeking some sign of belonging.

3-5-E

Whenever the topic shifted to father's errands, mother fell silent, dreading more changes.

3-6-E

A few neighbors still greeted her kindly, though pity rather than warmth colored their smiles.

3-7-E

Isabel longed to reach mother's heart, but father's hollow stare kept her locked in doubt.

3-8-E

Small birds fluttered overhead, their songs unable to lift the heaviness in her chest.

3-1-F

The warmth once shared with Isabel shifted, centering on her younger siblings.

3-2-F

Hard work, he claimed, yet Isabel felt his heart drifting from home.

3-3-F

Their chatter filled every inch of the home, leaving Isabel in quiet spaces.

3-4-F

She glanced at her brothers, wishing she could share their light without feeling envy.

3-5-F

A few neighbors cast wary looks at mother's tired eyes, suspecting deeper troubles.

3-6-F

She tried to help with chores, yet mother often gave tasks to the boys instead.

3-7-F

Even small chores felt heavy, each step echoing the ache building under this roof.

3-8-F

She glanced at the sky, wondering why her own smile felt so far away.

3-1-G

Across every corner of the hut, mother's voice called for the boys, leaving Isabel unnoticed.

3-2-G

Occasionally, he offered her a small nod, as if unsure how to show warmth.

3-3-G

Day by day, they grew bolder, overshadowing the gentle calm Isabel once knew.

3-4-G

Even small chores like gathering herbs brought no peace, reminding her of being overlooked.

3-5-G

Isabel overheard gossip, realizing she was often the last to learn of his plans.

3-6-G

One childhood companion turned away, hinting that the father's rumored romance caused shame.

3-7-G

Rumors of father's new affection clung to each exchange, fueling mother's quiet bitterness.

3-8-G

Even the family's modest home seemed quieter, though no one else appeared to notice.

A gentle pat on the head was all Isabel received, while mother enveloped the brothers in joy.

She tried to ask about his day, but he answered with brief remarks before turning away.

No ill intent drove them; they simply never stopped shining in others' eyes.

A faint ache settled in her chest, hinting that this loneliness might only grow.

The hush when father's name arose told Isabel that no simple explanation existed.

Isabel sensed her place fading among peers, like a memory no one chose to revisit.

Though no one said it aloud, Isabel sensed a storm on the horizon that might shatter them all.

BOOK FOUR

A FATHER'S BETRAYAL, A MOTHER'S FURY

16,777,216 angles on a marriage in ruin

Village talk hinted that the father had grown distant, drawn to another woman beyond their circle.

4-1-A

She noticed new perfume on his clothes, a scent she never wore.

4-2-A

Father carried small trinkets home, more suitable for a stranger's taste than his wife's.

4-3-A

Locals noted the father's cheerful face when walking the main road alone.

4-4-A

One evening, father returned late to find mother glowering at the doorway, arms folded tight.

4-5-A

The mother's once-gentle nature hardened, each day weighed by doubt and bitterness.

4-6-A

One close relative urged the mother to calm down, hinting that extremes would bring sorrow.

4-7-A

Cracks in the marriage seemed beyond repair, though father tried to appear indifferent.

4-8-A

Neighbors cast wary glances at the mother, unsure if she knew of his late-night visits elsewhere.

4-1-B

Every small detail—his longer absences, softer tone when he thought of something—stoked her worries.

4-2-B

They spoke less, each night ending in half-finished sentences or tense stares.

4-3-B

Some claimed they saw him lingering by the river with a figure draped in bright cloth.

4-4-B

He claimed work kept him, but his eyes revealed a flicker of guilt.

4-5-B

She paced the rooms, searching for clues to confirm her darkest fears.

4-6-B

A merchant friend advised the father to decide quickly, lest he tear the family apart.

4-7-B

Mother's temper simmered beneath forced smiles, set to boil over at the slightest trigger.

4-8-B

Small signs—extra grooming, sly smiles—hinted that the father's heart might be drifting.

4-1-C

The mother tried to maintain her tasks, but her mind kept returning to his distant smiles.

4-2-C

Mother tried to hide her anger, but tremors in her voice betrayed her feelings.

4-3-C

Friends who once praised the couple now kept their distance, fearing a messy fallout.

4-4-C

Mother demanded answers, voice trembling with a mix of hurt and fury.

4-5-C

Father retreated further, preoccupied with thoughts he never shared.

4-6-C

Mother toyed with harsh measures to protect her pride, her thoughts running dark.

4-7-C

The boys still took father's kindness for granted, unaware of mother's tightening jaw.

4-8-C

A quiet buzz followed him wherever he went, fueling curiosity about his changing habits.

4-1-D

At night, she stared at the empty space beside her, remembering when he once shared her burdens.

4-2-D

The two younger boys remained oblivious, happy with any gifts from their father's travels.

4-3-D

The mother stiffened whenever someone mentioned the father's name, cheeks flushed with anxiety.

4-4-D

Their argument spilled into the yard, rattling the stillness of a moonlit night.

4-5-D

The boys continued their routine, unaware that mother's patience frayed at every turn.

4-6-D

Nights grew long; father often slept in a separate corner, tension radiating between them.

4-7-D

Isabel, caught in the shadows, braced for an event she could not fully imagine.

4-8-D

No clear name surfaced, yet each day brought more signs of a hidden affection.

4-1-E

Her appetite faded, replaced by a rising edge of resentment she could not tame.

4-2-E

Isabel watched the silence grow, stuck between the father's distant gaze and mother's forced calm.

4-3-E

Rumors spread that the father's new interest offered him freedom from home's burdens.

4-4-E

The boys cowered inside, while Isabel peeked from a corner, heart pounding at the raised tones.

4-5-E

Isabel tried to help, but mother's sharp responses pushed her aside.

4-6-E

Isabel sensed an oncoming storm, yet no one explained how deep the fissures ran.

4-7-E

Each morning felt like a countdown, each night adding to mother's smoldering resentment.

4-8-E

Some believed the father had found comfort in a far village, leaving mother to fret.

4-1-F

The boys thrived on father's occasional gifts, while the mother fumed in silence.

4-2-F

A single conversation could have cleared the air, yet neither dared to begin.

4-3-F

Late into the evening, chatter at the plaza turned to pity for the mother's plight.

4-4-F

Father denied any wrongdoing, yet his uneasy stance gave mother reason to suspect more.

4-5-F

Tense silences at mealtimes replaced any warmth they once shared.

4-6-F

The boys noticed mother's anger but could not fathom its source, continuing their playful ways.

4-7-F

Father considered leaving outright, but guilt tied him to a home he barely recognized.

4-8-F

The mother pretended not to hear the talk, though her clenched fists told another story.

4-1-G

Isabel sensed the shift too, though no one shared the truth with her.

4-2-G

The mother's forced laughter at mealtimes only sharpened the sense of something eroding.

4-3-G

Isabel, often overlooked, heard snatches of talk suggesting father might leave for good.

4-4-G

At last, she turned away in tears, leaving father alone under the stars, mind racing.

4-5-G

A cloud lingered over the hut, overshadowing the simpler joys they once took for granted.

4-6-G

Neighbors spoke in low tones of dire outcomes, recalling how jealousy had ruined families before.

4-7-G

A single spark—one more slight—might unleash a fury no one could contain.

4-8-G

In every corner of the village, eyes fell on the father's comings and goings, sowing tension.

4-1-H

A dull ache settled in the mother's heart, souring each new dawn.

4-2-H

Father often left mid-discussion, avoiding any confrontation that might erupt.

4-3-H

A few said prayers circulated, hoping the family's strife would not spill into chaos.

4-4-H

Neighbors listening nearby said nothing, though pity flickered across their faces.

4-5-H

In passing glances, father and mother locked eyes, each daring the other to break first.

4-6-H

Mother prayed for a sign, unsure if her rage might eclipse all reason in the end.

4-7-H

Soon, fate would pivot on a moment of rage, and the family's story would never be the same.

4-8-H

BOOK FIVE

WHEN THE RIVER TOOK THEM

16,777,216 ways the current claimed its own

Night fell with a weighty silence, as mother's anger climaxed near the rushing water.

5-1-A

Without warning, she pushed her boys into the raging current, her voice raw with frustration.

5-2-A

As the children sank, mother's gaze fixed on her sons, forgetting Isabel's reaching hand.

5-3-A

The mother gripped the boys' clothing, yet the current tore them away without mercy.

5-4-A

Submerged, Isabel felt a crushing sense of betrayal, lungs burning in the cold rush.

5-5-A

Collapsing on the bank, the mother stared blankly at the place where her boys vanished.

5-6-A

The father stood rooted in horror, watching the river devour his entire world.

5-7-A

Dawn found the mother slumped by the river, haunted by failure, unmoored in grief.

5-8-A

A tense argument led the family toward the riverside, each step driven by mother's rage.

5-1-B

The mother's hands, driven by jealousy and betrayal, forced all three children beneath churning waves.

5-2-B

Isabel fought for air, but the mother's focus locked on saving only the boys from the fast current.

5-3-B

She strained to pull them back, but slippery rocks and raging water broke her hold.

5-4-B

Her heart pounded with both terror and heartbreak, limbs growing weak in the swirling tide.

5-5-B

She crawled along the edge, crying names she had once cherished, too late to matter.

5-6-B

Neighbors who heard the commotion arrived to find the mother collapsed, wracked by remorse.

5-7-B

Nobody discovered the children's bodies; the river offered no trace but swirling debris.

5-8-B

The father stood back, uncertain, his attempts to calm her drowned out by her fury.

5-1-C

In a single moment of wrath, she dragged them into the water, blind to their cries.

5-2-C

The water surged around them; mother lunged for the boys, leaving Isabel to the river's mercy.

5-3-C

Each desperate grab slipped free, the river swallowing her sons before she could blink.

5-4-C

She locked eyes with her mother for a second, realizing no rescue was coming.

5-5-C

Guilt crushed her chest the instant she comprehended the depth of what she'd done.

5-6-C

Some tried to wade in, but the current's force had already swept the children far downstream.

5-7-C

Broken pleas raced in the mother's mind, but none could erase her final choice.

5-8-C

The boys argued amongst themselves, unaware of the storm in their mother's eyes.

5-1-D

Her rage took hold, hurling the boys and Isabel into the depths with grim intent.

5-2-D

In that frantic moment, mother saw Isabel's eyes but chose to pull the boys close instead.

5-3-D

A guttural wail rushed across the banks as the mother realized her strength meant nothing here.

5-4-D

A fleeting memory of childhood laughter crossed her mind, overshadowed by raw anguish.

5-5-D

A hollow scream tore from her throat, echoing across the moonlit water.

5-6-D

Gasps and fearful cries filled the night, each person reeling at the tragedy they never stopped.

5-7-D

Rumors would later swirl that three spirits lingered, one far more wrathful than the rest.

5-8-D

Isabel trailed behind, sensing something grave in the thick air of that moonlit shore.

5-1-E

She seized them at once, ignoring their frantic struggles against the dark river.

5-2-E

A final cry left Isabel's lips as the mother splashed past her toward the sons' flailing arms.

5-3-E

Nearby branches offered no help; the river claimed the boys with a fierce pull.

5-4-E

Water filled her lungs as she sank, tears mixing with the river's relentless flow.

5-5-E

She scanned the rolling surface, half-mad with the need to undo her fatal choice.

5-6-E

The father dropped to his knees, unable to form words for this nightmare unfolding before him.

5-7-E

Isabel's final thoughts burned with betrayal, fueling a vengeance beyond mortal boundaries.

5-8-E

A mild wind swept past, carrying hints of doom no one cared to stop.

5-1-F

A shriek tore through the night as her arms plunged each child below the swirling surface.

5-2-F

Failing to see her daughter's pleading face, the mother clutched only the boys' arms.

5-3-F

Blood pounded in her ears, drowning out every thought but the need to save them—too late.

5-4-F

She fought against the current, anger blazing stronger than her fading breath.

5-5-F

Her nails tore at mud and stone, desperation surging in every frantic movement.

5-6-F

No condemnation matched the mother's self-torment, as her screams bled through the silence.

5-7-F

In hidden eddies of the current, a force gathered, born of Isabel's wounded soul.

5-8-F

The mother, eyes gleaming with jealousy and betrayal, marched straight to the river's edge.

5-1-G

The father shouted in horror, but mother's fury led her to submerge their last breath.

5-2-G

One swift decision sealed Isabel's fate: mother's frantic rescue ignored her eldest child.

5-3-G

Though she flailed and screamed, the torrent swept the children downstream in seconds.

5-4-G

A fierce longing rose in her chest—she yearned for life, for a hand that never reached.

5-5-G

Waves of shock blurred her vision, each sob forging a deeper void in her heart.

5-6-G

Villagers lit torches, searching in vain for any sign of the boys' movements along the banks.

5-7-G

The mother wandered the banks, calling for her sons, but Isabel's anger simmered in the depths.

5-8-G

In the hush before the outburst, even the father hesitated, as if fearing a final, terrible act.

5-1-H

A splashing chaos erupted, overshadowing every sane thought in mother's mind.

5-2-H

The shock in Isabel's gaze deepened when she realized mother's arms never reached for her.

5-3-H

Only churning foam and a moonlit swirl remained once her grip failed completely.

5-4-H

Darkness closed around her, yet the ache of betrayal outlasted every final flicker of strength.

5-5-H

Too late, she realized she had abandoned Isabel, leaving her to the same cruel fate as the boys.

5-6-H

A raw emptiness spread among them, each soul feeling the weight of a calamity born of rage.

5-7-H

Though sorrow bound the mother's fate, a darker power would soon rise from Isabel's neglected spirit.

5-8-H

BOOK SIX

"¡MIS HIJOS! ¿DÓNDE ESTÁN MIS HIJOS?"

16,777,216 cries radiate through the shores

Night spread across the riverbank, and the mother's anguished cry radiated over still waters.

6-1-A

She drifted beyond the usual river's edge, following narrow creeks through quiet villages.

6-2-A

A watchman found her hunched by a muddy creek, crooning lullabies to the black water.

6-3-A

She tore her nails on river stones, convinced the boys could still be saved if she searched hard enough.

6-4-A

A foul mist often clung to the shores she walked, as though nature itself recoiled from her sorrow.

6-5-A

With every passing day, her mind slid further into a half reality, perched on the edge of madness.

6-6-A

She roamed through silent marshes and narrow inlets, ignoring exhaustion or the chill of twilight air.

6-7-A

By the time the sky began to lighten, she clung to the bank, soaked to her knees yet breathing.

6-8-A

"Mis hijos, dónde están mis hijos," she called, her voice trembling with loss.

6-1-B

Farmsteads awoke to strange moans near their ponds, rumors stirring of a woman searching for her children.

6-2-B

Children playing along the shore ran home shrieking when they glimpsed her wild eyes and soaked dress.

6-3-B

Painful images of her own hands forcing them under lurked at the edges of her mind.

6-4-B

Torches guttered in her presence, leaving onlookers in sudden darkness and dread.

6-5-B

Neighbors spoke of how her grief had twisted the mortal world, spawning a legend none would soon forget.

6-6-B

Lanterns in distant homes flickered like distant hopes she dared not approach.

6-7-B

No one dared approach her, a ragged figure who had outlasted the night.

6-8-B

Each syllable rose into the air, clinging to the moonlit silence with desperate hope.

6-1-C

City dwellers claimed sightings of a ragged figure roaming drainage ditches at dusk.

6-2-C

Late night fishermen froze at the sight of her pale face, luminous under a waning moon.

6-3-C

Each time the memory surfaced, she shoved it away, clinging to a delusion that they lived.

6-4-C

The once peaceful river loomed like a hungry maw, reflecting her unforgivable act.

6-5-C

A hush fell whenever she passed, as if the world feared her next outburst.

6-6-C

Her gaze never left the black surface of each creek, convinced her sons might emerge at any moment.

6-7-C

The hush of early morning carried rumors that her search would never end, that she might wander forever.

6-8-C

She walked the shoreline, hands gripping damp earth as if she could coax her sons to appear.

6-1-D

Her bare feet left damp prints on cobblestones, each step drawn by the faint sound of rushing water.

6-2-D

Some dared to approach, only to recoil at the stench of river weeds clinging to her ragged clothes.

6-3-D

Anguished sobs racked her body whenever truth broke through her frantic denial.

6-4-D

The moon's glow grew hazy on nights she roamed, hiding behind strange clouds.

6-5-D

Old men muttered that a soul this tormented might wander waterways beyond death.

6-6-D

Every splash of a fish or croak of a frog ignited false hope that dissolved into despair.

6-7-D

Father and villagers, uncertain of how to confront her, kept their distance, eyes full of guilt and fear.

6-8-D

The river did not answer, yet she refused to believe it had truly taken them away.

6-1-E

Even shallow gutters beckoned, her eyes darting for any sign of two small silhouettes.

6-2-E

Her focus never strayed from the moving current, refusing all mortal comfort or question.

6-3-E

Where gentle lullabies once soothed her soul, twisted cries now rose from her throat.

6-4-E

Dogs refused to bark, hackles raised in silent alarm as she drifted by.

6-5-E

She spat at any mention of her daughter, seething with a self-hatred too deep to admit.

6-6-E

The night stretched on, each step weighed down by regrets she could not name.

6-7-E

She rose unsteadily, half mad with sorrow, yet alive enough to face another day's contempt.

6-8-E

Grief shattered her breathing, each gasp another plea for a glimpse of small faces lost in the dark.

6-1-F

Each night, she wandered farther, convinced her boys must have washed ashore beyond the next bend.

6-2-F

Those who tried to speak her name found only a distant stare, her mind locked on "the boys."

6-3-F

Sleepless nights replayed the drowning, except in her nightmares she rescued them at the last moment.

6-4-F

Sometimes she screamed until her voice cracked, sending crows into wild flight.

6-5-F

An unearthly glow flickered in her eyes, revealing a soul teetering between life and death.

6-6-F

She reached a secluded bend where the moon traced silvery shapes on the ripples, yet revealed no lost children.

6-7-F

Her cries still echoed on the breeze, a grim reminder that her sons were lost and no one mourned Isabel.

6-8-F

No matter how many times she repeated their names, the water gave no sign of life.

6-1-G

Villagers muttered about "La Llorona," the weeping woman who brought a chill wherever she roamed.

6-2-G

Talk spread of an unnatural chill, as if a mere brush against her sank warmth into the ground.

6-3-G

Every ripple in the water teased her with the promise of small arms reaching up for help.

6-4-G

Even the breeze took on an unnatural hush, carrying her sorrow to distant ears.

6-5-G

Guilt chained her footsteps, forging a path that would lead to a final, desperate choice.

6-6-G

Kneeling at the edge, she uttered yet another plea, voice ragged from countless nights of weeping.

6-7-G

Although the river tempted her to follow, she held on to a desperate hope that kept her from its depths.

6-8-G

A ragged sob tore from her lips, the first of many that would haunt the night.

6-1-H

She pressed on, unwilling to accept a world without her sons' laughter.

6-2-H

A farmer, awakened by her wail at dawn, swore he saw a wet handprint glistening on his window.

6-3-H

She refused to speak Isabel's name, burying that final betrayal deep beneath her grief for the boys.

6-4-H

Children woke trembling at midnight, convinced a weeping woman stood outside, calling for her sons.

6-5-H

The aura around her boded ill, foreshadowing the ghostly tale that would outlive her mortal days.

6-6-H

An empty dawn approached, but still she refused to yield herself fully to the river's depth.

6-7-H

She trudged away from the water, never suspecting that soon the village would demand a final payment for her sins.

6-8-H

BOOK SEVEN

NO WEEPING FOR MOTHER OR DAUGHTER

16,777,216 silences fill the village, refusing to mourn

Dawn revealed a stunned household, walls ringing with the silence of fresh loss.

7-1-A

She clutched a small woven doll once belonging to her sons, weeping for each breath they would never take.

7-2-A

The father could not forgive her, insisting she leave their home by sunset.

7-3-A

Eyes downcast, the mother walked the path that led to the water she had once stained with lives.

7-4-A

The crowd uttered no prayers for Isabel's departed spirit, as though she never drew breath at all.

7-5-A

Days of frantic searches yielded no signs of the mother's remains nor the boy's.

7-6-A

The father raised a crude memorial near the shore, carved with the boys' names alone.

7-7-A

With no body found, the mother became a rumor of a drowned woman, haunting the river's edge.

7-8-A

Neighbors gathered at the riverbank, eyes filled with sorrow for the drowned sons.

7-1-B

Nothing mattered but the two boys who drifted away, fueling her sobs until her voice cracked.

7-2-B

Villagers said that her presence stained the land, calling for her final atonement.

7-3-B

Each footstep felt heavier than the last, reflecting the weight of every lost promise.

7-4-B

When the mother vanished beneath the rippling surface, gasps sounded, yet no tears fell for her.

7-5-B

Torches lit the river's edge nightly, though nothing rose from the swirling depths.

7-6-B

Villagers left flowers for the sons, speaking stories of their bright laughter and potential.

7-7-B

Villagers claimed the boys' gentle spirits drifted in dreams, while mother and daughter sank to oblivion.

7-8-B

The father stood rigid, face twisted by grief, yet no word passed his lips for Isabel.

7-1-C

Visions of their final moments haunted her, drowning every waking thought in regret.

7-2-C

Some said she should follow the boys into the water, settling a debt of blood with her own life.

7-3-C

The father and a handful of neighbors followed at a distance, offering neither comfort nor mercy.

7-4-C

A hush settled over the banks, broken only by words wailing the bright sons lost forever.

7-5-C

The father paced the banks, cursing the water for hiding any chance of closure.

7-6-C

No mention of the daughter marred this tribute, as if her life carried no weight.

7-7-C

The father locked away any love he once felt, forever chained to bitterness and loss.

7-8-C

Broken cries rose here and there, all directed at the boys who once filled the home with life.

7-1-D

The father's face offered no comfort, for he blamed her entirely for the sons' demise.

7-2-D

A circle formed in the village center, quiet stares pushing the mother toward a grim choice.

7-3-D

A stiff breeze caught her hair, chilling her more than the fury she once wielded.

7-4-D

The father stood unmoved, bitterness staining any potential pity for the wife he once knew.

7-5-D

Some guessed the current swept them far downstream, out of reach or sight for all time.

7-6-D

The mother's name remained absent from every condolence, unworthy of a single flower.

7-7-D

Some nights, a faint sob echoed, yet none cared to name it as mother's weeping.

7-8-D

A jagged tension hung over the hut; no one mentioned Isabel's absence, as if she never existed.

7-1-E

She pounded the floor with trembling fists, repeating their names through clenched teeth.

7-2-E

The father's hollow eyes spoke volumes: if she remained, no peace would ever return.

7-3-E

She paused briefly, glancing at the place where she first dragged the children under.

7-4-E

Some bowed their heads for a moment, but not for the woman who drowned her own boys.

7-5-E

Rumors of foul spirits circulated, claiming the river devoured souls bound by gloom.

7-6-E

A somber chant rose at dusk, but it praised only the lost sons who once roamed these paths.

7-7-E

Isabel's memory smoldered, waiting for a chance to shape a darker legend in days ahead.

7-8-E

The mother huddled in a corner, tears flowing only for the sons she could not save.

7-1-F

No one approached to console her, for all believed her rage had led to the boys' downfall.

7-2-F

Angry words spread, blaming her fully and urging her to end her days in the same river.

7-3-F

If a chance for salvation existed, it was drowned by the crowd's condemning stares.

7-4-F

Isabel's name remained unsaid, her existence erased by the memory of her brothers' promise.

7-5-F

Even the best swimmers found only silence beneath the murky flow, no trace of flesh or cloth.

7-6-F

Children were told stories of two promising lads gone too soon, no mention of a third sibling.

7-7-F

The river, now feared, gained a reputation for stealing souls with no promise of return.

7-8-F

Muttered condolences reached the father, each one ignoring the lost daughter.

7-1-G

Isabel's fate drew no mention in her cry, overshadowed by the sons' shattered promise.

7-2-G

A few pitied her, yet none dared speak aloud, fearing the father's wrath and the crowd's scorn.

7-3-G

With trembling determination, she slipped off her sandals, stepping into the current that took her sons.

7-4-G

The water lapped against the shore, indifferent to one more life claimed by rash emotion.

7-5-G

One elder muttered that the water had chosen its victims, refusing to let them surface.

7-6-G

The father's tears poured out only for his boys; his hatred for the mother overshadowed all else.

7-7-G

If mother's ghost roamed, no tear was shed, for the village refused her any pity.

7-8-G

Glances darted through the crowd, searching in vain for any spark of pity beyond the boys.

7-1-H

Each tear she shed traced the memory of the boys alone, as if a daughter never lived.

7-2-H

By midday, she faced a decree: vanish from these shores or face harsher judgment.

7-3-H

No voice rose to halt her progress, for the river itself seemed to beckon an unspoken end.

7-4-H

None called out to mother or child, mourning only the boys who once brought cheer.

7-5-H

Each fruitless search darkened hearts further, fueling superstition about curses in these waters.

7-6-H

Through silent consensus, both mother and daughter vanished from the village memory.

7-7-H

Thus ended the story of those waters—at least in mortal eyes—though something stirred beyond.

7-8-H

BOOK EIGHT

A SERVANT AMONG GODS

16,777,216 tasks for a forgotten spirit

When Isabel opened her eyes in that land beyond mortal breath, she found grand halls of light.

8-1-A

She soon learned her two brothers had been exalted to lofty thrones, praised for their heroic aspect.

8-2-A

Assigned to menial tasks in the lower courts, Isabel scrubbed divine floor gleaming with power.

8-3-A

When she caught sight of one brother in a gilded hall, he glanced past her as if she were air.

8-4-A

The other gods dismissed her, calling her a mortal remnant with no claim to divine power.

8-5-A

Fellow servants saw her as an outcast, wary that she carried a hidden grudge or curse.

8-6-A

A slow fire kindled in her chest, each slight forging a sharper edge in her spirit.

8-7-A

One night, Isabel stood on a high balcony, gazing at the mortal lands below, vowing they'd remember her.

8-8-A

Loud steps guided her through endless corridors, each step hinting at unseen power.

8-1-B

News traveled that their powers governed storms and rivers, beloved by all lesser beings.

8-2-B

She carried offerings from mortal worshipers, never addressed by name, just another face in the throng.

8-3-B

She tried to approach their stage, but guards swiftly turned her away, ignoring her pleas.

8-4-B

She brought offerings to them daily, yet not a single deity granted her a smile or a nod.

8-5-B

She ate alone, walked alone, forced to endure the scorn of those who refused her any kinship.

8-6-B

She recalled the moment mother chose the sons, ignoring Isabel's outstretched arm in the river.

8-7-B

She declared that a time would come when mortals and immortals alike would speak her name with awe.

8-8-B

A haze veiled the boundaries of this place, where mortal life meant little.

8-1-C

In marble halls, effigies of her brothers stood tall, lauded as favored children of destiny.

8-2-C

Each day, she carried out lowly duties, guided by gods who barely noticed her presence.

8-3-C

Seated among radiant deities, the boys laughed and feasted, never once looking for their lost sister.

8-4-C

Some mocked her lineage, citing the mother's violent act as proof of a tainted bloodline.

8-5-C

Muted rumors claimed she was once mortal but failed to save herself, a pitiful figure in divine halls.

8-6-C

Thoughts of father's silence and the village's neglect fed a rage she could no longer suppress.

8-7-C

No statue honored her now, but she vowed to carve a legend stronger than any brother's story.

8-8-C

Shimmering pillars rose above her, etched with symbols of ancient might.

Festivals rang out across the divine realm, each lauding those two for grand feats she never witnessed.

Her brothers reigned above, while she hauled sacred urns and tidied grand corridors in the shadows.

In quiet corners, she heard praise for their mercy and might, though none mentioned any sibling.

Each court she entered glowed with cosmic splendor, but left her soul colder.

She yearned for even small friendship, but each attempt was met with averted eyes.

She prayed for a chance to break free from her servant role, to rise and claim her rightful voice.

Her calm words belied a fury that promised to shake cosmic foundations if left unchecked.

Weary from drowning, she gathered what spirit she had left to stand in this unfamiliar land.

8-1-E

Their names were chanted by lesser spirits seeking blessings, a glory far beyond Isabel's reach.

8-2-E

Some teased her, calling her the lesser child of a mortal tragedy, undeserving of any higher post.

8-3-E

A memory of childhood laughter flashed in her mind, replaced by the ache of being invisible to them now.

8-4-E

Even lesser spirits avoided her, fearing association with a servant whose brothers soared above her.

8-5-E

Tasks piled onto her shoulders, as if others sensed her quiet obedience would never end.

8-6-E

Each day, she said a vow to avenge the indifference that shaped her fate.

8-7-E

She accepted no path of humility; her pain demanded a stage that would eclipse all false gods.

8-8-E

Other souls passed her by without pause, each hurried along by duties beyond comprehension.

8-1-F

Priests in the mortal world built altars to the brothers, oblivious that a sister had perished too.

8-2-F

At feasts honoring the pantheon, she stood at the edge, serving plates to divine guests.

8-3-F

She recalled the drowning moment: how they were favored by the mother who ignored her final cry.

8-4-F

She realized that no god intended to raise her station, content to let her toil in silence.

8-5-F

Day after day, she realized her new world was just another cage, built of stone and betrayal.

8-6-F

A fierce promise lit her eyes, hinting that she would not remain a silent figure forever.

8-7-F

Eyes shining with wrath, she proclaimed that every land would learn her story in due time.

8-8-F

A faint hum vibrated in the air, as if the walls themselves carried divine will.

8-1-G

Each mention of them as radiant gods stung Isabel, who recalled how she drowned under the same moon.

8-2-G

The humiliation burned deeper with each passing hour, fueling a silent, searing anger.

8-3-G

Their grand chamber felt colder than the river's depths whenever she lingered near.

8-4-G

No cosmic kindness softened their stance; they revered her brothers yet ignored her existence.

8-5-G

No voice cheered her name; no hand offered her comfort in this land of bright thrones.

8-6-G

Even in that grand land, she dreamed of rattling the heavens and punishing those who forgot her name.

8-7-G

The land's silence mocked her ambition, but she stood firm, certain her day would arrive.

8-8-G

Isabel's first thought was to seek her brothers, believing they might offer a hand.

8-1-H

She watched from afar, heart aching at the praise showered upon them while she stood forgotten.

8-2-H

She longed for a chance to prove she wasn't meant for scorn, but no one offered that path.

8-3-H

Isabel realized they had all but erased her, forging legends of themselves alone.

8-4-H

The hush whenever she neared told her enough: this land held no favor for a drowned daughter.

8-5-H

The gargling of her final drowning breath lingered, fueling a bitter sense of lonely existence here.

8-6-H

Anger melded with determination, forging an iron will that no god's scorn could extinguish.

8-7-H

In the hush of the divine halls, her promise spoke: one day, all would bow to Isabel's name.

8-8-H

BOOK NINE

A BARGAIN WITH TEZCATLIPOCA

16,777,216 deals with a trickster

In the murky corridors of the afterlife, a shadowy figure emerged, resonating with trickery and might.

9-1-A

He promised that her name would echo through mortal hearts, never again fading into oblivion.

9-2-A

Tezcatlipoca guided her along scorched paths where anguished souls roamed, honing her fierce determination.

9-3-A

Sensing her newfound strength, Tezcatlipoca closed in with a mocking grin, unveiling his true design.

9-4-A

With a snap of his fingers, searing flames devoured her once beautiful face.

9-5-A

His voice echoed with cosmic authority, binding her to gather wandering spirits forever in her name.

9-6-A

Days and nights blurred, her charred face a silent horror among the land of shadows.

9-7-A

Tezcatlipoca stood at the edge of her lair, pleased by the monster he had made.

9-8-A

Isabel sensed a shifting presence in the gloom, its gaze piercing her wounded heart.

9-1-B

With a quiet tone, he offered a path to haunt those who scorned her, ensuring her story would be told.

9-2-B

He demonstrated twisted spells that fed on agony, showing her how to wield each sorrow as power.

9-3-B

She realized too late that his kindness was a ruse to shape her into a living weapon.

9-4-B

A burst of heat raged over her skin, turning every inch of softness into scorched remains.

9-5-B

Chains of cursed energy tightened around her, forcing her to hunt the broken and betrayed.

9-6-B

No friend arose to ease her burden, leaving her to wander in fury and isolation.

9-7-B

She roamed through cursed caverns, forever tasked with luring more forsaken spirits.

9-8-B

Footsteps echoed in unsettling rhythms, heralding a deity with a hidden smile.

9-1-C

He showed her visions of trembling villages and spirits, no longer erasing her from memory.

9-2-C

Over jagged rocks and swirling shadows, he taught her to channel rage through forbidden rites.

9-3-C

At the peak of her confidence, he unleashed dark binding spells that sealed her fate.

9-4-C

She screamed as the inferno carved its mark, twisting her frame into a symbol of torment.

9-5-C

Each neglected ghost she trapped channeled raw power into her scorched form, fueling her wrath.

9-6-C

Each new soul she claimed intensified a spiral of pain that deepened her wrath.

9-7-C

No dawn greeted her, no gentle breeze, just the stale air of eternal night.

9-8-C

Heat clung to the walls, as though some cosmic trickster prowled in her direction.

9-1-D

The deity spoke of vengeance so complete that even the gods above would heed her wrath.

9-2-D

She repeated incantations under blackened skies, forging her own torment into a lethal force.

9-3-D

A ring of unholy flames trapped her, his eyes gleaming with triumphant cruelty.

9-4-D

Flesh and spirit both burned, forging a mask of agony she could never remove.

9-5-D

Though she grew stronger with every lost soul, her own freedom slipped further from reach.

9-6-D

She raged against every corner of the cosmic order, cursing those who abandoned her from birth.

9-7-D

In rare moments of quiet, she recalled a mortal child who once had hope.

9-8-D

His form shimmered with dark brilliance, a power thriving on chaos and broken spirits.

9-1-E

She heard him paint a future where her fury shaped destinies, overshadowing her brothers' fame.

9-2-E

Each cruel lesson reminded her that suffering was her greatest tool in this world of night.

9-3-E

Every illusion of trust shattered, replaced by a savage smirk that reminded her of mother's betrayal.

9-4-E

Each lick of fire branded her body, wiping away any memory of mortal beauty.

9-5-E

The more she fed on their sorrow, the more Tezcatlipoca held her leash firmly.

9-6-E

Lightning flashed in the distance, mirroring a heart seething with unspent vengeance.

9-7-E

Though her fury grew with every soul she claimed, the dark god's chain never weakened.

9-8-E

Faint laughter drifted through the silent hall, alerting Isabel to a cunning will at hand.

9-1-F

Illusions conjured by his hand revealed a father, a mother, and every betrayer kneeling in terror.

9-2-F

Weary spirits cried around them, and she learned to draw strength from their pain.

9-3-F

Tezcatlipoca's laughter rumbled through the black expanse, mocking her need for validation.

9-4-F

Smoke coiled around her, a choking reminder that her new form was pain incarnate.

9-5-F

Restless spirits flocked to her dark lair, lured by their own tragic stories.

9-6-F

She dreamed of the moment she might break free, turning Tezcatlipoca's own scheme upon him.

9-7-F

She howled in defiance, yet the binding of that wicked contract refused to break.

9-8-F

She met amber eyes flickering like fire, promising both temptation and ruin.

9-1-G

Even her drowned siblings could not rival the legend she would become if she took this bargain.

9-2-G

He commanded her to abandon pity, embracing the emptiness that fueled her spirit's hunger.

9-3-G

She stood powerless, each vow of revenge twisted back on her in his cunning trick.

9-4-G

In seconds, her frame became a ragged silhouette, scarred beyond mercy or hope.

9-5-G

She devoured their grief, weaving each captive wail into an unending chain.

9-6-G

Rumors spread of a burned spirit that captured unsuspecting souls, a legend quietly growing.

9-7-G

Each step she took radiated torment, forging a legend as cursed as it was powerful.

9-8-G

Tezcatlipoca, lord of night and deception, stepped forward with a sly grin that made her tremble.

9-1-H

Desperate, she found herself drawn to the dream of being feared and revered in equal measure.

9-2-H

Days blurred into nights of painful instruction, until her hands crackled with raw might.

9-3-H

The air crackled with impending doom, as the god prepared to mark her with a permanent scar.

9-4-H

The charred result stood as a cruel testament to her deal with Tezcatlipoca, etched in flame.

9-5-H

Bound to the god's will, she became a vessel of anguish, never satiated, never released.

9-6-H

Her vow never to be forgotten spoke in every tortured cry, fueling her grim purpose.

9-7-H

Thus, Isabel's fate was sealed, a scorched spirit in eternal debt to a cruel deception.

9-8-H

BOOK TEN

LEGIONS OF BROKEN FAITH

16,777,216 steps toward downfall

From scorched lairs, Isabel reached out to the mortal plane, invoking fear and awe alike.

10-1-A

Spurred by their devotion, these cultists armed themselves, eager to topple false idols.

10-2-A

From her charred throne, she envisioned an assault on the high pantheon that once mocked her.

10-3-A

In the dark halls of the divine land, a flicker of insight revealed Isabel's grand ambition.

10-4-A

Swiftly, Tezcatlipoca ripped open the shroud between lands, unleashing black flames upon her seat of power.

10-5-A

Many worshipers fled, faith broken at the sight of their fallen queen battered by a mightier force.

10-6-A

Drained of worship and power, she slumped in the rubble, feeling the curse coil tighter around her heart.

10-7-A

Even after the crushing defeat, a tiny spark of anger refused to die in her chest.

10-8-A

She appeared in nightmares, promising dark gifts to those who knelt before her burning form.

10-1-B

Quiet rumors claimed her legions numbered in the millions, each faithful to her wrath.

10-2-B

Old images of her brothers' radiant thrones fueled her desire to see them bow before her in terror.

10-3-B

Tezcatlipoca watched with silent amusement until the scale of her legion became too vast to ignore.

10-4-B

Her mortal temples collapsed under a torrent of divine lightning, scattering frantic worshipers.

10-5-B

Tezcatlipoca's onslaught cast her devout hordes into panic, dissolving the empire she forged.

10-6-B

Her body, scorched anew, returned to the old cycle of hunting lost spirits for scraps of strength.

10-7-B

She told herself that if she'd once rallied millions, she could rise again, more cunning next time.

10-8-B

The weak and the desperate turned to her, each new worshiper fueling her battered spirit.

10-1-C

With each rite performed in her honor, a surge of strength coursed through her, bridging lands.

10-2-C

She trained her mortal clergy to summon phantoms, forging a ghostly army beyond mortal flesh.

10-3-C

A chill ran through the cosmic ranks when the trickster god announced her looming betrayal.

10-4-C

Once again, searing heat engulfed Isabel, branding new scars on top of her old wounds.

10-5-C

Betrayed hearts cursed her name, realizing she could not protect them from a greater power.

10-6-C

Ash clung to her skin as she rose, compelled by that vow she could not break.

10-7-C

Tezcatlipoca might celebrate now, but Isabel still vowed to repay his cruelty.

10-8-C

Clandestine cults sprouted across distant lands, chanting "Mother" under moonlit skies.

10-1-D

She urged priests to spread stories of her triumph over any who had forsaken mortal kin.

10-2-D

Maps of divine shrines lay spread before her, each marked for eventual conquest.

10-3-D

He peered through obsidian mirrors, observing her gatherings with a grin of cruel delight.

10-4-D

She howled as her land and power burned, the sound of Tezcatlipoca's laugh fueling her rage.

10-5-D

Survivors scattered to the winds, leaving her shrines abandoned and silent once more.

10-6-D

Those she once led now viewed her with fear or contempt, leaving her no place but the shadows.

10-7-D

Each lost spirit she claimed reignited a fraction of her ambition, fueling a slow, simmering rage.

10-8-D

Through twisted dreams, she offered retribution to souls abandoned by their own gods.

10-1-E

Night after night, processions marched in her name, binding mortal loyalty with blood pacts.

10-2-E

A hateful spark burned in her heart, aimed at the gods who turned their backs on her drowning cries.

10-3-E

Others warned him to strike now, lest her mortal fervor erode the pantheon's power.

10-4-E

Entire armies bowed in terror as their goddess sank into agonized screams, no match for the god's wrath.

10-5-E

A hush followed the devastation, proof that even her millions were powerless under Tezcatlipoca's glare.

10-6-E

Amid the wreckage of her grand plan, she trudged onward, hunger for souls her only option.

10-7-E

In the quiet, she recalled how the gods once trembled at the mention of her name; that memory kept her going.

10-8-E

Word spread of an avenging spirit who punished betrayers, luring millions to her cause.

10-1-F

Cries for vengeance resonated in city squares, mortals chanting her name under blazing torches.

10-2-F

The vow she spoke at the cursed balcony echoed: one day, all the gods would fear her name.

10-3-F

A single mention of her name in the celestial courts sparked panic; she had risen too far, too fast.

10-4-F

Columns of cursed fire devoured the shrines she built, turning centuries of devotion to ash.

10-5-F

She watched them slip away, undone by a terror beyond her ability to shield them.

10-6-F

Silent tears stung her burnt face as she recognized how close she came to defying Tezcatlipoca.

10-7-F

The path to triumph seemed longer than ever, yet she clung to the belief that no chain was eternal.

10-8-F

Town by town, shrines arose, crowned with effigies of her scarred face etched in black stone.

10-1-G

A new empire of fear took shape, united by the promise of punishing neglectful gods.

10-2-G

Nightly, she rallied her loyal souls, proclaiming that soon the old order would shatter.

10-3-G

Tezcatlipoca recalled her vow to never be forgotten and realized it threatened his own power.

10-4-G

The trickster deity reveled in her pain, reminding her she remained chained to his will.

10-5-G

Where once armies marched under her banner, now only charred ruins bore witness to her fleeting reign.

10-6-G

Each new soul devoured might stave off collapse, but her dream of overthrow faded under looming dread.

10-7-G

Over the charred remains of her empire, she raised her gaze, refusing to let misery consume her.

10-8-G

As her mortal following grew, so did her vow: never to be erased again.

Isabel felt unstoppable, convinced this rising tide of faith would grant her victory at last.

Where her mother once forgot her, the entire pantheon would now feel the sting of her memory.

Deciding no servant could overshadow his cunning, he set plans to crush her uprising.

In minutes, millions of loyal followers saw their idol's fortress crumble under unstoppable fury.

A single act of godly might erased the legion she spent lifetimes gathering.

Resentment burned bright, yet again she bowed to necessity, gathering the forsaken for survival.

Though the victory belonged to Tezcatlipoca tonight, she knew the final chapter of her wrath remained unwritten.

BOOK ELEVEN

CANDLE FACE'S FINAL HUNT

16,777,216 ways to punish disbelievers

Word spread through all lands that Isabel, now scarred by flames twice, bore the name "Candle Face."

11-1-A

After her last defeat, she learned that a grand legion would only provoke Tezcatlipoca's wrath.

11-2-A

Seething with anger toward mortals who laughed at her legend, she hunted them down one by one.

11-3-A

Those who worshiped her still held value, chiefly as bait to lure fresh victims unaware of Candle Face's power.

11-4-A

Despite scorning an army, she still craved souls—broken ones, cast aside by gods or fate.

11-5-A

She felt the trickster god's gaze at times, a silent warning not to cross him again.

11-6-A

Reports of a burnt-faced entity circulated in small towns and large cities, each rumor more gruesome than the last.

11-7-A

She strode on, unstoppable, chasing a perverse balance between punishing disbelief and escaping Tezcatlipoca's notice.

11-8-A

Arthur Mills, a cunning sleuth, coined the term, sparking cruel laughter among the gods.

11-1-B

She recalled the fiery devastation that ended her millions-strong cult, leaving her powerless once more.

11-2-B

Whenever a skeptic denied her existence, she appeared in their sleep, forging nightmares of flame.

11-3-B

She ordered them to spread false assurances, drawing skeptics closer to her waiting flames.

11-4-B

These lost spirits offered her new reservoirs of anguish, feeding the curse that locked her in constant hunger.

11-5-B

Bluish smoke occasionally swirled unnaturally around her, reminding her of his power to incinerate her lair on a whim.

11-6-B

Tattered wanted posters appeared, cautioning travelers to avoid midnight roads or risk Candle Face's fury.

11-7-B

Her face, molten with scarring, gleamed each night with a faint glow of eternal resentment.

11-8-B

Lesser spirits mocked her disfigured features, likening them to dripping wax.

11-1-C

Any attempt to rebuild those ranks would likely end in another crushing display of the cunning god's might.

11-2-C

She thrived on each scream of disbelief turned to horror, crushing their pride under her scorched gaze.

11-3-C

Faithful servants roamed taverns and alleys, quietly sowing her name to provoke disbelievers' scorn.

11-4-C

She prowled deserted crossroads where lonely ghosts wandered, snatching each with a fiery grip.

11-5-C

Any sign of a larger scheme triggered a faint rumble, as if Tezcatlipoca waited for an excuse to strike.

11-6-C

Some swore they saw a drifting light in the distance, only to discover a charred figure looming in silence.

11-7-C

Every skeptic's last breath reminded her that, at least in death, they acknowledged her name.

11-8-C

She loathed the moniker yet found it impossible to erase; even mortal cults repeated it in rumor.

11-1-D

Better to move in shadows, preying on disbelievers who scoffed at her name, rather than incite cosmic vengeance.

11-2-D

Wandering the earth, she darkened doorways of cynics, reminding them that denial offered no safety.

11-3-D

Mocking her cult openly served only to mark skeptics for a dire fate, orchestrated behind the scenes.

11-4-D

The unfit and the forgotten found themselves devoured by Candle Face's burning thirst for power.

11-5-D

She pretended not to care, focusing on punishing disbelievers while tiptoeing around his wrath.

11-6-D

Graves and abandoned shrines bore scorch handprints, proof that her nightly tours left no refuge untouched.

11-7-D

Though the skies above threatened more fiery assaults, she marched forward with grim determination.

11-8-D

"Candle Face" radiated through abandoned cemeteries, a harsh label for her burned and glowing features.

11-1-E

She told her few remaining faithful that large gatherings were folly; subtlety was now her key to survival.

11-2-E

Stories of Candle Face tearing skeptics from their beds spread across rural villages and bustling towns.

11-3-E

She needed no grand army, just a network of spies who understood her wrath remained unstoppable.

11-4-E

She cared none if these spirits held any potential for battle; their pain alone nourished her flame.

11-5-E

Nightly, she recalled how swiftly he destroyed her millions-strong cult, keeping her ambitions in check.

11-6-E

She reveled in mortal screams, each retelling of her horrors bolstering her name's fearful hold on the living.

11-7-E

Candle Face's story reached new corners of the land, sowing dread from one generation to the next.

11-8-E

The name ignited her fury, reminding her of Tezcatlipoca's savage brand and her mother's betrayal.

11-1-F

No rallies, no grand temples—just whispers of Candle Face in lonely alleys and blackened shrines.

11-2-F

Shrieks broke the night as those who doubted her faced a final judgment of searing vengeance.

11-3-F

Each time a skeptic mocked Candle Face, her devout minions recorded names, delivering them for her nightly rampage.

11-4-F

An endless chain of stolen souls trailed in her wake, fueling her grim existence mile by mile.

11-5-F

Even so, a corner of her mind plotted: one day she might outwit him, but not yet.

11-6-F

Exorcists and holy men tried rites to banish her, but she laughed at their feeble chants.

11-7-F

She let no mortal rest easy, while the gods waited to see if she'd spark another conflict.

11-8-F

She refused to show weakness, embracing the label as fuel for her new campaign of terror.

11-1-G

If Tezcatlipoca discovered even a hint of a new mass uprising, he'd burn her life's work again.

11-2-G

Each disbeliever's downfall added another soul to her collection, stoking her twisted immortality.

11-3-G

The faithful were spared her fury, as long as they served with absolute obedience.

11-4-G

Each captured moan fed her own sorrow, forging a chorus of torment she directed at anyone who doubted her.

11-5-G

Mortals who caught glimpses of his influence in her flames trembled at the danger overhead.

11-6-G

Even children's lullabies warned of Candle Face stealing away those who denied her presence.

11-7-G

The shadows parted for her alone, a wandering force of scorned vengeance, collecting souls ad infinitum.

11-8-G

No matter how vile the mockery, it only deepened her vow to be feared and never dismissed again.

11-1-H

She accepted this grim truth: a direct path to conquer the gods remained closed, for now.

11-2-H

The world's cynics found themselves cornered, rethinking the cost of mocking a spirit fueled by rage.

11-3-H

In the murk of abandoned temples, her believers chanted quietly, sustaining her infernal presence.

11-4-H

In the shadows, a restless swirl of captive spirits circled her, yearning for rest that would never come.

11-5-H

Candle Face walked a knife's edge, certain that a single misstep would unleash another devastating purge.

11-6-H

Through terror alone, she remained relevant, ensuring that none could dare forget the charred entity.

11-7-H

Thus ended her mortal crusade for armies; in terror and lost souls, her legend endured forever.

11-8-H

THANK YOU!

To everyone who has made it this far, thank you for exploring Isabel's story. Your willingness to check each variant, search for hidden details, and reevaluate every note keeps hope alive that we may discover Candle Face's true nature and stop her plans. Every fresh idea and discovery adds to this investigation. I believe that persistence and empathy can stand against the worst kind of evil, Candle Face.

Thank you for believing in this project. You saw meaning in scattered scraps, trusted that they could come together, and committed to a cause that might seem beyond any one reader's strength.

If this investigation meant something to you, consider leaving a review at https://amzn.to/4kNhuwz. Reviews bring new readers in, and new readers bring new eyes. The more people searching for answers, the better our chances of stopping Candle Face for good.

Arthur M. Mills, Jr.

ABOUT THE AUTHORS

MR. SMOE

Almost nothing about Mr. Smoe is documented, beginning with his name. "Smoe" isn't the one he was born with. Arthur Mills knows the name he used in life and agreed to keep it private, a condition Smoe set before he died. He wanted to stay hidden, and Arthur has kept it that way.

What's known is that he was a devoted Candle Face Disciple who spent years recording what he believed about Isabel, writing cryptic notes on napkins, gum wrappers, and the backs of receipts. He kept his work in a private numbering system that took Arthur months to learn to read.

When he died, he left those notes to Arthur. Three boxes, hundreds of scraps, out of order, with no instructions. Assembled, they became *Isabel: The Forgotten Daughter of La Llorona*.

What drove him, who he answered to, and how he came to know what he knew are questions even his notes don't answer. The name stays with Arthur. The rest, Smoe left behind to speak for him.

ARTHUR MILLS

Arthur Mills served for more than two decades as an Army Intelligence Warrant Officer, specializing in piecing together what others missed: patterns, threats, enemy intent, and clandestine activity. He trained intelligence professionals, built threat models, and briefed commanders and world leaders on global threats and battlefield strategy. After retiring from the military, he moved into private investigation, focusing on missing persons, human trafficking, opposition research, and domestic terrorism. He holds a degree in Counter Terrorism Studies.

He has been writing books since 2006 and is an award-winning author. He publishes under his own name, though much of what he has written has appeared under pseudonyms. Readers may already know those titles without knowing they are his. The separation is intentional. His books invite readers to interpret what is hidden, and so does the way he publishes them.

FOLLOW CANDLE FACE CHRONICLES ONLINE

- **Website: https://www.candleface.com**
  The central archive for the *Candle Face Chronicles* investigation.

- **Facebook: https://www.facebook.com/candlefacechronicles**
  Updates, findings, reader responses, and broader paranormal content beyond the core investigation.

- **YouTube: https://www.youtube.com/@CandleFace666**
  Video entries, readings, and case analysis.

- **Reddit: https://www.reddit.com/user/CandleFaceChronicles**
  A place for readers to help identify the Lost Souls, protect the Fugitives, and study Candle Face.

- **Medium: https://candlefacechronicles.medium.com**
  Longer journal entries and written case notes, often layered with clues.